A Note to Parents and Caregivers:

Read-it! Readers are for children who are just starting on the amazing road to reading. These beautiful books support both the acquisition of reading skills and the love of books.

The PURPLE LEVEL presents basic topics and objects using high frequency words and simple language patterns.

The RED LEVEL presents familiar topics using common words and repeating sentence patterns.

The BLUE LEVEL presents new ideas using a larger vocabulary and varied sentence structure.

The YELLOW LEVEL presents more challenging ideas, a broad vocabulary, and wide variety in sentence structure.

The GREEN LEVEL presents more complex ideas, an extended vocabulary range, and expanded language structures.

The ORANGE LEVEL presents a wide range of ideas and concepts using challenging vocabulary and complex language structures.

When sharing a book with your child, read in short stretches, pausing often to talk about the pictures. Have your child turn the pages and point to the pictures and familiar words. And be sure to reread favorite stories or parts of stories.

There is no right or wrong way to share books with children. Find time to read with your child, and pass on the legacy of literacy.

Adria F. Klein, Ph.D.
Professor Emeritus
California State University
San Bernardino, California

For Galen Engholm, the happiest big kid I know—J.K.

Editor: Jacqueline A. Wolfe
Designer: Joe Anderson
Page Production: Angela Kilmer
Creative Director: Keith Griffin
Managing Editor: Catherine Neitge
The illustrations in this book are prepared digitally

Picture Window Books
5115 Excelsior Boulevard
Suite 232
Minneapolis, MN 55416
877-845-8392
www.picturewindowbooks.com

Printed in the United States of America.

Library of Congress Cataloging-in-Publication Data
Kalz, Jill.
Galen's camera / by Jill Kalz ; illustrated by Ji Sun Lee.
p. cm. — (Read-it! readers)
Summary: Young Galen views ordinary objects from a different perspective through the
eye of his camera.
ISBN 1-4048-1610-0 (hard cover)
[1. Visual perception—Fiction. 2. Cameras—Fiction.] I. Lee, Ji Sun, ill. II. Title.
III. Series.

PZ7.K12655Gal 2005
[E]—dc22   2005023153

Galen's Camera

by Jill Kalz
illustrated by Ji Sun Lee

Special thanks to our advisers for their expertise:

Adria F. Klein, Ph.D.
Professor Emeritus, California State University
San Bernardino, California

Susan Kesselring, M.A.
Literacy Educator
Rosemount–Apple Valley–Eagan (Minnesota) School District

PiCTURE WiNDOW BOOKS
Minneapolis, Minnesota

Galen has three eyes—two in his
head and one in his hands.

Galen sees many things
with these two eyes.

But he sees even more with this one.

Galen sees his dad's shoelace.

It looks like a long, white worm.

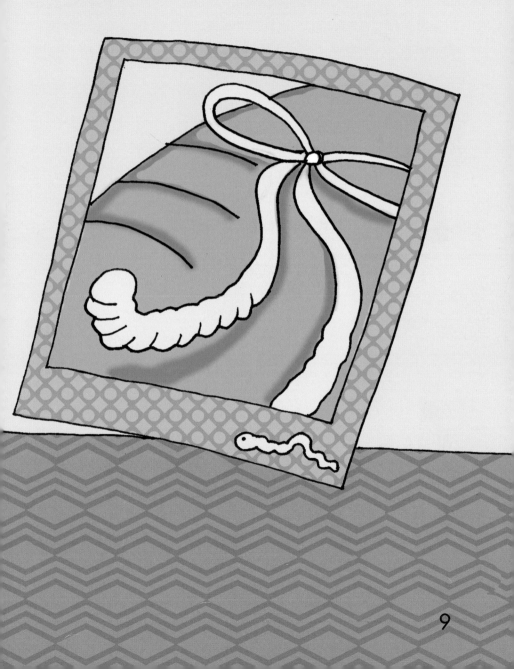

He sees his puppy's nose.

It looks like a sugar-coated gumdrop.

He sees inside the refrigerator.

It looks like a colorful painting.

He sees his older sister.

She always looks the same.

He sees bed sheets drying
in the wind.

They look like pink and yellow ghosts.

He sees a flock of geese.

It looks like his finger.

Sometimes, Galen sees
a happy little kid.

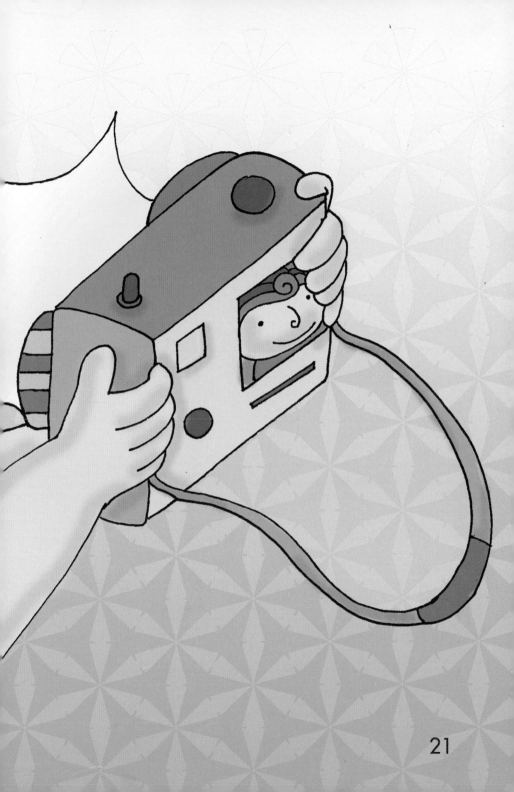

He looks a lot like Galen!

More *Read-it!* Readers

Bright pictures and fun stories help you practice your reading skills. Look for more books at your level.

At the Beach 1-4048-0651-2
Bears on Ice 1-4048-1577-5
The Bossy Rooster 1-4048-0051-4
Dust Bunnies 1-4048-1168-0
Flying with Oliver 1-4048-1583-X
Frog Pajama Party 1-4048-1170-2
Jack's Party 1-4048-0060-3
The Lifeguard 1-4048-1584-8
Mike's Night-light 1-4048-1726-3
The Playground Snake 1-4048-0556-7
Recycled! 1-4048-0068-9
Robin's New Glasses 1-4048-1587-2
The Sassy Monkey 1-4048-0058-1
Tuckerbean 1-4048-1591-0
What's Bugging Pamela? 1-4048-1189-3

Looking for a specific title or level? A complete list of *Read-it!* Readers is available on our Web site:
www.picturewindowbooks.com